The Dog Who Cried Wolf

KEIKO KASZA

PUFFIN BOOKS

This book is dedicated to Kyoka.

And a special thanks to the real Moka,
Moka Latham-Brown, the pet dog of my friends.
His lively personality was the inspiration for the book.

PUFFIN BOOKS
Published by the Penguin Group
Penguin Young Readers Group, 345 Hudson Street, New York, New York 10014, U.S.A.
Penguin Group (Canada), 90 Eglinton Avenue East, Suite 700, Toronto, Ontario, Canada M4P 2Y3
(a division of Pearson Penguin Canada Inc.)
Penguin Books Ltd, 80 Strand, London WC2R 0RL, England
Penguin Ireland, 25 St Stephen's Green, Dublin 2, Ireland
(a division of Penguin Books Ltd)
Penguin Group (Australia), 250 Camberwell Road, Camberwell, Victoria 3124, Australia
(a division of Pearson Australia Group Pty Ltd)
Penguin Books India Pvt Ltd, 11 Community Centre, Panchsheel Park,
New Delhi - 110 017, India
Penguin Group (NZ), 67 Apollo Drive, Rosedale, North Shore 0632, New Zealand
(a division of Pearson New Zealand Ltd)
Penguin Books (South Africa) (Pty) Ltd, 24 Sturdee Avenue, Rosebank, Johannesburg 2196, South Africa

Registered Offices: Penguin Books Ltd, 80 Strand, London WC2R 0RL, England

First published in the United States of America by G. P. Putnam's Sons, a division of Penguin Young Readers Group, 2005
Published by Puffin Books, a division of Penguin Young Readers Group, 2009

7 9 10 8

THE LIBRARY OF CONGRESS HAS CATALOGED THE G. P. PUTNAM'S SONS EDITION AS FOLLOWS:
Kasza, Keiko.
The dog who cried wolf / Keiko Kasza.
p. cm.
Summary: Tired of being a house pet, Moka the dog moves to the mountains to become a wolf but soon misses the comforts of home.
ISBN: 978-0-399-24247-2 (hc)
[1. Dogs—Fiction. 2. Wolves—Fiction.] I. Title.
PZ7.K15645Mk 2005 [E]—dc22 2004024737

Puffin Books ISBN 978-0-14-241305-0

Design by Gunta Alexander.
Text set in Angie.

Manufactured in China

Moka was a good dog. He and Michelle loved to be together. Life was perfect, until one day, she read a book about wolves.

"Look, Moka," said Michelle, "you're kind of like a wolf!"

Wow! thought Moka. I *am* kind of like a wolf. But look how amazing wolves are! They run around free, hunt wild animals, and stay up late to howl at the moon.

DOG FOOD
MOKA

And look at the way I live, Moka sighed. I'm nothing but a house pet. He felt like a failure, especially when Michelle made him dress up for her tea parties. He wanted to be a wolf.

The next day, Moka made up his mind. He snuck out of the house and took off for the mountains. He ran, and ran, and ran . . .

. . . until finally he reached a high mountaintop.
“I’m free!” he yelped. “Free as a wolf!”

He ran.

He jumped.

He danced.

And he peed wherever he wanted.

"Wow!" he exclaimed. "The world is mine!"

Soon, Moka got hungry. “No problem!” he cried. “I’ll hunt for my food, just like the wolves do.”

And off he went.

But a rabbit outran him.

A skunk sprayed him.

A beetle pinched him.

And even a field mouse
made fun of him.

By nightfall, Moka was miserable. He missed Michelle.
"I even miss her tea parties," he mumbled. "But I can't
give up yet. There is just one more thing I have to try . . ."

He gazed at the golden moon and howled as loudly as he could: “Haooooooooo . . . ,” just like a wolf.

Suddenly, something howled back! "Haoooooooo . . . Haooooooo . . ." and then again, "Haoooooo . . ."

Moka froze.

"Wooooooooolves!" he cried. "Real wolves!"

He turned and raced down the mountain. "I want to go home!" he panted. "I never want to be a wolf again!"

He ran, and ran, and ran . . .

MAIL
Missing Dog!
Answers to Moka
Call Michelle
at

. . . until finally he reached the house he knew so well.

"Moka!" Michelle shouted as she dashed out to meet him.

"You're back!"

FISH

Moka was home again, and he and Michelle were oh, so happy! Life was just perfect, until one day, she read a book about monkeys. . . .